EUROPEAN COUNTRIES TODAY
POLAND

EUROPEAN COUNTRIES TODAY

TITLES IN THE SERIES

Austria	Italy
Belgium	Netherlands
Czech Republic	Poland
Denmark	Portugal
France	Spain
Germany	Sweden
Greece	United Kingdom
Ireland	European Union Facts & Figures

EUROPEAN COUNTRIES TODAY
POLAND

Dominic J. Ainsley

Mason Crest
450 Parkway Drive, Suite D
Broomall, Pennsylvania PA 19008
(866) MCP-BOOK (toll free)

Copyright © 2019 by Mason Crest, an imprint of National Highlights, Inc. All rights reserved. No part of this publication may be reproduced or transmitted in any form or by any means, electronic or mechanical, including photocopying, recording, taping, or any information storage and retrieval system, without permission in writing from the publisher.

First printing
9 8 7 6 5 4 3 2 1

ISBN: 978-1-4222-3989-6
Series ISBN: 978-1-4222-3977-3
ebook ISBN: 978-1-4222-7804-8

Cataloging-in-Publication Data on file with the Library of Congress.

Printed in the United States of America

Cover images
Main: *The churches of St. Stanislaw and St. Vaclav and Wawel Castle, Kraków.*
Left: *Borscht (beetroot) soup.*
Center: *Monument to the Warsaw Uprising of World War II.*
Right: *A walker in the Tatra Mountains.*

QR CODES AND LINKS TO THIRD-PARTY CONTENT

You may gain access to certain third-party content ("Third- Party Sites") by scanning and using the QR Codes that appear in this publication (the "QR Codes"). We do not operate or control in any respect any information, products, or services on such Third-Party Sites linked to by us via the QR Codes included in this publication, and we assume no responsibility for any materials you may access using the QR Codes. Your use of the QR Codes may be subject to terms, limitations, or restrictions set forth in the applicable terms of use or otherwise established by the owners of the Third-Party Sites. Our linking to such Third-Party Sites via the QR Codes does not imply an endorsement or sponsorship of such Third-Party Sites or the information, products, or services offered on or through the Third-Party Sites, nor does it imply an endorsement or sponsorship of this publication by the owners of such Third-Party Sites.

CONTENTS

Poland at a Glance	6
Chapter 1: Poland's Geography & Landscape	11
Chapter 2: The Government & History of Poland	21
Chapter 3: The Polish Economy	43
Chapter 4: Citizens of Poland: People, Customs & Culture	53
Chapter 5: The Famous Cities of Poland	67
Chapter 6: A Bright Future for Poland	83
Chronology	90
Further Reading & Internet Resources	91
Index	92
Picture Credits & Author	96

KEY ICONS TO LOOK FOR:

Words to Understand: These words with their easy-to-understand definitions will increase the reader's understanding of the text while building vocabulary skills.

Sidebars: This boxed material within the main text allows readers to build knowledge, gain insights, explore possibilities, and broaden their perspectives by weaving together additional information to provide realistic and holistic perspectives.

Educational Videos: Readers can view videos by scanning our QR codes, providing them with additional content to supplement the text. Examples include news coverage, moments in history, speeches, iconic sports moments, and much more!

Text-Dependent Questions: These questions send the reader back to the text for more careful attention to the evidence presented there.

Research Projects: Readers are pointed toward areas of further inquiry connected to each chapter. Suggestions are provided for projects that encourage deeper research and analysis.

POLAND AT A GLANCE

MAP OF EUROPE

The Geography of Poland

Location: central Europe, east of Germany
Area: (about twice the size of Georgia; slightly smaller than New Mexico)
  total: 120,727 square miles (312,685 sq. km)
  land: 117,473 square miles (304,255 sq. km)
  water: 3,254 square miles (8,430 sq. km)
Borders: Belarus 259 miles (418 km), Czech Republic 494 miles (796 km), Germany 290 miles (467 km), Lithuania 64 miles (104 km), Russia (Kaliningrad Oblast) 130 miles (210 km), Slovakia 336 miles (541 km), Ukraine 332 miles (535 km)
Climate: temperate with cold, cloudy, moderately severe winters with frequent precipitation; mild summers with frequent showers and thundershowers
Terrain: west and south mostly mountains (Alps); east and north flat or gently sloping
Elevation extremes:
  lowest point: near Raczki Elbląskie -7 feet (-2 m)
  highest point: Rysy 8,199 feet (2,499 m)
Natural hazards: flooding

Source: www.cia.gov 2017

POLAND AT A GLANCE

Flag of Poland

Poland's position in Europe goes a long way to explain its complex and varied history. With constant invasions from neighboring countries, it has been partitioned several times and re-founded twice in this century. Poland was the first satellite country of the Soviet Union to bring down its Communist regime, which encouraged many other Eastern European countries to follow suit. The colors of the flag derive from those of the Polish coat of arms (a white eagle on a red field), which dates back to the thirteenth century. The flag, using red and white, was first used in 1919. Since 1989, when anti-Communists took over, it has been a popular notion that the colors stand for peace (white) and socialism (red).

ABOVE: *The Jewish quarter of Kraków is full of bars, restaurants, and cafés.*

EUROPEAN COUNTRIES TODAY: POLAND

The People of Poland

Population: 38,476,269
Ethnic Groups: Polish 96.9%, Silesian 1.1%, German 0.2%, Ukrainian 0.1%, other and unspecified 1.7%
Age Structure:
  0–14 years: 14.76%
  15–24 years: 10.7%
  25–54 years: 43.48%
  55–64 years: 14.21%
  65 years and over: 16.86%
Population Growth Rate: -0.13%
Birth Rate: 9.5 births/1,000 population
Death Rate: 10.4 deaths/1,000 population
Migration Rate: -0.4 migrants/1,000 population (2016 est.)
Infant Mortality Rate: 4.4 deaths/1,000 live births
Life Expectancy at Birth:
  Total Population: 77.8 years
  Male: 73.9 years
  Female: 81.8 years
Total Fertility Rate: 1.35 children born/woman
Religions: Catholic 87.2%, Protestant 0.4%, Muslim 4.2%, Orthodox 1.3%, other 0.4%
Languages: Polish (official) 98.2%, Silesian 1.4%, other 1.1%, unspecified 1.3%
Literacy rate: 99.8%

Source: www.cia.gov 2017

Words to Understand

capital city: A city or town that is the official seat of government in a country.

coastal plain: A plain extending along a coast.

continental climate: A climate characterized by hot summers, cold winters, and little rainfall, typical of the interior of a continent.

BELOW: The Stawa Młyny is a beacon in the stylized shape of a windmill in Świnoujście, a town on the Baltic Sea. The beacon acts as navigational aid for vessels entering the port of Świnoujście. It was built between 1873 and 1874.

Chapter One
POLAND'S GEOGRAPHY & LANDSCAPE

Welcome to Poland, one of the largest countries in Central Europe. Bordered by Russia, Lithuania, Belarus, Ukraine, Slovakia, the Czech Republic, Germany, and the Baltic Sea, Poland and its culture have been shaped by its central location and the ease with which people, ideas, and even armies have moved across the area.

Poland is the eighth-largest country in Europe, covering 120,727 square miles (312,685 sq. kilometers). Most of this area is low lying, although there are some mountains to the south. The Baltic Sea lies to the north and provides Poland with easy access to Scandinavian and North Sea ports. Warsaw, the capital city, is situated in the center of the country, on the Wisła River.

A Sandy Coast, Rolling Plains, and Mountains

Stretching from coastal plains to mountain ranges, Poland can be divided into three major natural land regions—the Baltic coastal plain in the north, lowlands in the center, and mountains in the south.

The Baltic coastal plain is a low, flatland mass that lies along the Baltic Sea, extending across Poland from Germany to Russia. Marshlands, dunes, and tidal flats—coastal areas alternately flooded and drained by the tides—dot the coastline.

The region immediately south of the coastal plain is relatively flat. This low-lying region is marked by thousands of lakes. More than 6,300 lakes are scattered across it. Wide river valleys divide the area into three sections—the Pomeranian Lakeland, the Masurian Lakeland, and the Great Poland Lakeland.

POLAND'S GEOGRAPHY & LANDSCAPE

Educational Video

A short video giving a brief insight into Poland's geography. Scan the QR code with your phone to watch!

ABOVE: The Tatra Mountains are in the Carpathians, which border Slovakia. In Poland, the mountains are situated in the Tatra National Park.

EUROPEAN COUNTRIES TODAY: POLAND

ABOVE: *One of the many lakes in the Masurian Lakeland, which is a haven for birds.*

As these rivers cut through the lowlands, they provide fertile land for cultivation. The farmland of the plain is critical to Polish agriculture. Many Polish cities have developed along these riverbanks. Some of these cities have become important industrial and commercial centers.

South of the central lowlands are the uplands of Little Poland. This region is marked by striking upthrusts of ancient rock, rich in minerals and coal. The coal, iron, zinc, and lead deposits found and mined here, near the old capital city of Kraków, had led to the growth of Poland's most important industrial region. The southernmost region of Poland is characterized by two mountain ranges, the Sudeten and the Carpathians along the border with the Czech Republic and

POLAND'S GEOGRAPHY & LANDSCAPE

ABOVE: The Sudeten mountain range stretches from eastern Germany to southwestern Poland and to the northern Czech Republic.

Slovakia. The Sudeten Range is somewhat smaller and features several granite quarries, while the Carpathians contain deposits of salt, sulfur, natural gas, and petroleum.

Rivers and Waterways

Poland is home to a number of interconnected rivers, canals, and lakes. Over the centuries, many of Poland's largest cities have developed along these water routes.

The most important river is the Wisła. Both a tourist river and a busy transport waterway, it flows from Slovakia in the south to the Baltic Sea in the north. The Odra is another river vital for transport, industry, and agriculture.

EUROPEAN COUNTRIES TODAY: POLAND

A Temperate Climate

Poland has a moderate, continental climate that is highly variable. Because of its nearness to the sea, Poland is affected by oceanic air masses from the west, cold air fronts from Scandinavia and the polar regions, and warmer air from the south. Instead of the more traditional four seasons, six different seasonal periods occur in Poland: a cold snowy winter lasting for as little as one or as many as three months, then a cold but drier period of alternating wintry and warmer weather, followed by a traditional sunny spring. Summers are warmer with abundant rain and sunshine, followed by a sunny fall. A cool, foggy period of humid weather signals the approach of winter.

ABOVE: *Warsaw is the capital of Poland. The city sits on the banks of the Wisła River.*

POLAND'S GEOGRAPHY & LANDSCAPE

ABOVE: The white stork is a common sight in Poland.

EUROPEAN COUNTRIES TODAY: POLAND

Eurasian Lynx

The Eurasian or European lynx is a medium-sized cat native to Europe. It is the third-largest predator after the brown bear and gray wolf. It is the largest of the four lynx species and a strict carnivore, consuming two or three pounds (one or two kg) of meat every day. This extremely efficient hunter uses fine-tuned stealth and pounce techniques to bring down animals four times its size, delivering a fatal bite to the neck or snout of an unsuspecting deer. During winter, its variably patterned coat is long and dense and large fur-covered paws help it move through deep snow. The Eurasian lynx is an endangered species. It can be found in Poland, but in small numbers. Its main threat is hunting and habitat loss.

Source: http://www.bbc.co.uk/nature/life/Eurasian_Lynx

Trees, Plants, and Wildlife

Nearly 20 percent of Poland is comprised of grassy plains and meadows. An additional 27 percent is covered with forest. Add this to the marshlands and coastal habitats near the Baltic Sea, and the mountainous regions in the south, and it is obvious why Poland is home to such a great variety of plants and wildlife.

Many migratory birds flock to Poland each year. Some of these include the highly endangered corncrake, which has been driven out of most areas of Europe due to intensive farming practices. The white stork also calls Poland home, with more of these birds found in Poland than in any other country

17

POLAND'S GEOGRAPHY & LANDSCAPE

in the world. Recent studies suggest that one in every four storks in the world is Polish.

Several different birds of prey also make their home in Poland. Among these, the white-tailed eagle is perhaps the best known; with its impressive wingspan of almost 8 feet (2.4 meters) and a sitting height of up to 36 inches (0.9 meters), this is a predator to be reckoned with. Other birds of prey include the greater spotted eagle, European honey buzzard, and the Eurasian hobby. The

ABOVE: *The impressive wingspan of a European honey buzzard in flight.*

EUROPEAN COUNTRIES TODAY: POLAND

Nietoperek Bat Preserve, located in an abandoned World War II bunker system, is home to some of the rarest bat species in the world, including the barbastelle, the natterer's bat, and the brown long-eared bat.

The world's largest remaining concentration of European bison can be found in Poland's protected wildlife areas. The country is also home to a significant number of other large mammals, including the European elk, the grey wolf, and the European lynx.

Currently, Poland maintains twenty-three different national parks to protect its wealth of natural treasures. Poland's government, just as it has for centuries, places the richness and variety of its lands as a priority.

Text-Dependent Questions

1. What are the three Polish lakeland areas called?

2. How many seasons does Poland have?

3. What species of eagles can be found in Poland?

Research Project

Draw a map of Poland. List all of the rivers, lakes, seas, and cities of Poland and then indicate them on your map.

19

Words to Understand

Huns: Members of a nomadic central Asian people who controlled large parts of central and eastern Europe in about 450 CE.

Magyars: Members of the predominant ethnic group of Hungary.

Slavic: A group of related languages that includes Russian, Bulgarian, Czech, Polish, etc.

BELOW: Ogrodzieniec Castle is a ruined castle in the highland region of the Polish Jura, in south-central Poland. Although rebuilt several times in its history, the medieval castle was originally built in the fourteenth and fifteenth centuries by the Włodkowie Sulimczycy family.

Chapter Two
THE GOVERNMENT & HISTORY OF POLAND

Poland has not always existed as the country it is today. For centuries, the nation suffered under the domination of foreign powers and the hardships of war. Today, Poland stands as a united, democratic country and a new member of NATO and the European Union (EU). Poland is committed to peace and building good relations with other countries. However, Poland has traveled a long road to reach its current state.

Early Poland
Ancient artifacts discovered on Polish lands suggest the area was home to Neanderthals and ancient tribal groups of hunter-gatherers. The area became more populated after the collapse of the Roman Empire as tribes from the south and west began to settle the area, probably seeking fertile farmland and freedom from the attacks of eastern tribes such as the **Huns** and **Magyars**.

By the tenth century, about twenty small states had been formed by various tribes. These groups included the Vistulans, Obodrites, Lendians, and Goplans. The most prominent group was the Polanes, or "People of the Plain," who settled the flatlands that still form the heart of Poland today. Originally a part of the Czech tribe, the Polanes eventually established themselves as a separate ethnic group, and in time became the largest **Slavic** group. The region settled by the Polanes has been known as Poland ever since.

The Middle Ages
In neighboring Germany, Otto I, a strong Saxon emperor, founded the Holy Roman Empire in 962 CE. The Holy Roman Empire was a group of western and central European territories that were united by faith in the Roman Catholic

THE GOVERNMENT & HISTORY OF POLAND

Educational Video

A time line video about the history of Poland.

Church. While there was only one emperor, each territory had its own individual ruler, appointed by the emperor.

In 966, Otto I granted the title of duke to Mieszko I, the leader of the Polanes. In exchange, the Polanes swore allegiance to the empire and began to convert the population to Christianity. By the time Mieszko died in 972, a strong alliance with the empire had been established, a substantial amount of additional land had been conquered, and conversion to Roman Catholicism was nearly complete. Mieszko's son Bolesław continued his father's work and was crowned king of Poland by the emperor shortly before his death in 1025. The Kingdom of Poland was established and became one of the major powers in eastern Europe.

In the centuries that followed, power shifted hands between different hereditary rulers as the kingdom faced

ABOVE: *A replica of the Magdeburger Reiter, which depicts King Otto I.*

EUROPEAN COUNTRIES TODAY: POLAND

intermittent warfare; some areas were lost to foreign invasion, while from time to time, new areas came under Polish rule.

As the Middle Ages progressed, Poland saw a great influx of settlers from the west, mainly Germans who brought valuable skills and new ideas. The Germans also brought with them their legal practices, which, being considered more sophisticated than traditional Polish practices, were widely adopted. Poland, now with a feudal system firmly established, Roman Catholicism as the dominant faith, and Germanic customs and law becoming common practice, had become a fully integrated part of medieval Europe.

Although Poland now had firmly established ties to Western Europe, there were many important differences

ABOVE: *Mieszko I of Poland and his son Bolesław I Chrobry.*

between life in medieval Poland and the remainder of western Europe. Germans were not the only immigrants to move east during this period. Large numbers of European Jews, persecuted during the Crusades, migrated to Poland as well. Poland welcomed these settlers and extended every protection of the law to the Jews. This included heavy penalties for the destruction of Jewish cemeteries and synagogues. Other important differences between Poland and the rest of feudal Europe included greater freedoms for the peasantry and a larger class of nobles in Poland (nearly 10 percent of the population by some estimates) than in other areas of Europe. These differences helped fuel the rapid development of cities and commerce and set the stage for a new era of growth and prosperity.

THE GOVERNMENT & HISTORY OF POLAND

Dating Systems and Their Meaning

You might be accustomed to seeing dates expressed with the abbreviations BC or AD, as in the year 1000 BC or the year AD 1900. For centuries, this dating system has been the most common in the Western world. However, since BC and AD are based on Christianity (BC stands for Before Christ and AD stands for anno Domini, Latin for "in the year of our Lord"), many people now prefer to use abbreviations that people from all religions can be comfortable using. The abbreviations BCE (meaning Before Common Era) and CE (meaning Common Era) mark time in the same way (for example, 1000 BC is the same year as 1000 BCE, and AD 1900 is the same year as 1900 CE), but BCE and CE do not have the same religious overtones as BC and AD.

ABOVE: *Poland protected the Jews who migrated to Poland during the Crusades. Anyone caught causing damage in a Jewish cemetery was severely punished.*

EUROPEAN COUNTRIES TODAY: POLAND

Poland's Golden Age

By the end of the fourteenth century, Poland was still a relatively thriving nation despite political upheavals and periodic warfare. Seeking to improve political conditions, acquire new lands, and enhance its military strength, Poland made a successful alliance with neighboring Lithuania. Lithuania was strong militarily and ruled large expanses of land to the east, including what is modern-day Belarus and parts of Ukraine. As a condition of the alliance, Lithuania converted to Roman Catholicism, and over the next century the resulting Jagiellonian dynasty (named for King Jagiełło, the first king of Poland-Lithuania, who also ruled under the name Władysław II) acquired land, wealth, and power.

ABOVE: *Władysław II Jagiełło, king of Poland.*

The success of the Jagiellonian dynasty can be traced to the distinctive features of its government, which was unlike the other European governments of the time. The large, landowning nobility had enough wealth and power to keep royal control in balance. Over time, a parliament was established, known as the Sejm, that was made up entirely of the nobility and had the power to pass laws, address grievances against the throne, and ultimately a monarch. Although the Jagiellonians were a hereditary ruling family, they eventually began to expand the power of the Sejm as a means of ensuring their heirs would be elected as successors.

The result of this shared power was one of the most enlightened states to exist in Europe at the time. As other countries were torn apart by the religious strife caused by the Protestant Reformation, Poland enjoyed relative religious freedom. Although the majority of the country was solidly Roman Catholic, religious dissent was well tolerated, and Poland became a haven for Lutherans,

THE GOVERNMENT & HISTORY OF POLAND

Calvinists, and other religious groups being persecuted elsewhere. By the late sixteenth century, Poland also supported the world's largest population of Jews, who now had a thriving culture of their own and were prospering as bankers and business managers. Poland was ethnically and linguistically diverse as

ABOVE: *Jagiellonian University (University of Kraków). Founded in 1364, by Casimir III the Great, the Jagiellonian University is the oldest university in Poland, the second-oldest university in Central Europe, and one of the oldest surviving universities in the world. Famous students include mathematician and astronomer Nicolaus Copernicus, Polish king John III Sobieski, Pope John Paul II, and Nobel laureates Ivo Andrić and Wisława Szymborska.*

EUROPEAN COUNTRIES TODAY: POLAND

well, with ethnic Poles, Germans, Czechs, Slovaks, Belorussians, Ukrainians, and Lithuanians coexisting peacefully. Most ethnic Poles at the time were members of the nobility, who governed a mass of peasantry whose roots were not Polish or even wholly Catholic. Ultimately, however, this imbalance would result in ethnic conflict.

In the meantime, literature, music, and the arts thrived in this environment of prosperity and freedom. The Polish nobility commissioned works heavily influenced by the popular Italian styles of the late Renaissance. Italian-style architecture also flourished, and many examples are still visible in the old capital city of Kraków. The University of Kraków (Jagiellonian University) gained prominence as a world-class center of learning, and, in 1543, Nicolaus Copernicus became its most famous student as he revolutionized the study of astronomy forever.

Modern Poles remember this era as the golden age of Polish culture and identify their national love of freedom and democracy as originating in this period. While the large noble class and the middle class consisting of merchants, bankers, and skilled craftsmen did enjoy relative freedom and civil liberty, the large peasant class, however, still remained virtual slaves to the land they worked.

After the last Jagiellonian ruler died without a male heir, the government gradually evolved into the Polish-Lithuanian Commonwealth, or Noble's Commonwealth. The monarchy's central power eroded until ultimately the country was governed completely by the legislature. Certain provisions in the constitution that allowed small groups of nobles to disrupt parliamentary procedures completely caused problems.

As the country faced external military

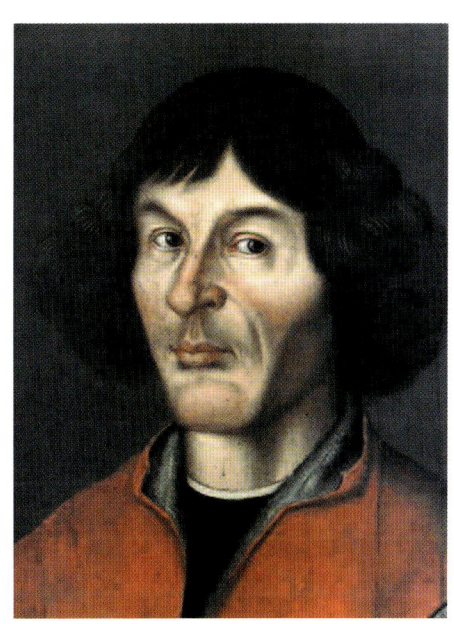

ABOVE: *Nicolaus Copernicus.*

THE GOVERNMENT & HISTORY OF POLAND

ABOVE: Napoleon Bonaparte *by Jacques Louis David.*

threats and internal power struggles, the government eventually deteriorated. Over time, land was lost to Sweden, Russia, and the Ottoman Turks. Eventually, Poland came completely under the control of Russia.

Nationalism and Romanticism

In 1795, Poland was subject to the last of three partitions, where the neighboring powers of Russia, Prussia, and Austria completely divided the territory of Poland and wiped the Polish-Lithuanian Commonwealth from the map. While much of Europe condemned this action as a crime against Polish sovereignty, no country came forward to actively oppose the annexation. By the dawn of the nineteenth century, however, new military developments encouraged Poles that their independence might one day be restored.

The French general Napoleon Bonaparte launched a series of aggressions and captured large portions of Europe. By 1806, he had dissolved Germany's Holy Roman Empire completely. The defeat awakened a sense of nationalism in the German territories. They banded together to fight against the French for Prussia, the largest German state. Poland's location in the center of Europe became very significant, and Napoleon promised to help restore an

EUROPEAN COUNTRIES TODAY: POLAND

ABOVE: *Stanisław II Augustus was king of Poland, grand duke of Lithuania, and the last monarch of the Polish-Lithuanian Commonwealth.*

THE GOVERNMENT & HISTORY OF POLAND

independent Poland—and he did in fact restore some autonomy to the Duchy of Warsaw. Although short lived, the Napoleonic era served as inspiration among intellectuals to show that a free and independent Poland was possible.

The artistic and intellectual climate of the day fueled the growth of nationalist movements in Poland. Nationalist movements swelled in popularity across Europe, and the artistic movement known as Romanticism was a natural inspiration for this movement. Romanticism idealized patriotism and ethnic loyalty, and promoted resistance against the conservative monarchies that imposed foreign rule on subject peoples across the continent. Arts and literature once again flourished, this time highlighting nationalist themes praising the glorious national past.

By the mid-nineteenth century, nationalist rebellions were occurring across Polish lands. The revolts were put down harshly, and action was taken to limit the use of Polish cultural practices and the language. Nationalist feelings also brought ethnic tensions, and conflict arose between ethnic Germans, Poles, and Jews. As World War I approached, many different political groups were promoting Polish nationalism and independence.

World War I and the Polish Republic

World War I began on June 28, 1914, when Gavrilo Princip, a Serbian nationalist, assassinated Austrian archduke Franz Ferdinand and his wife, Sophie. Russia allied with Serbia. Germany sided with Austria and soon declared war on Russia. After France declared its support for Russia, Germany attacked France. German troops then invaded Belgium, a neutral country, since it stood between German forces and Paris. Great Britain then declared war on Germany. As one of

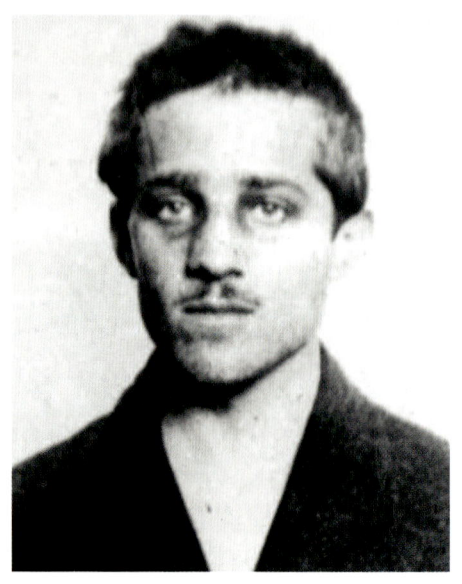

ABOVE: Gavrilo Princip.

EUROPEAN COUNTRIES TODAY: POLAND

ABOVE: *Archduke Franz Ferdinand.*

THE GOVERNMENT & HISTORY OF POLAND

ABOVE: *In 1934, Hitler became Germany's head of state, with the title of* Führer und Reichskanzler *(Leader and Chancellor of the Reich).*

the Allies, Poland also entered the war.

1918, a newly independent Poland emerged, but it faced many great economic and political challenges. The new nation dealt with almost constant border disputes as boundaries were moved and redrawn across Central Europe following the war. The infant nation also had to contend with staggering amounts of war damage, a ruined economy, and dissatisfied minority groups who made up one-third of the country's total population.

Nazi Germany and World War II

Despite the multitude of internal problems, the greatest threat to Poland came from abroad. Poland allied itself with France for protection against both Nazi Germany and Soviet Russia. Poland also sought to further secure its position by signing nonaggression treaties with Germany and Russia.

Poland felt threatened because Germany was gaining power and rebuilding its military under the leadership of Adolph Hitler. In 1936, he formed an alliance with Italy and signed an anti-Communist agreement with Japan. These three powers became known as the Axis Powers. France, Great Britain, and the countries that were allied with them became known simply as "the Allies."

Hitler's stated goals of reclaiming German lands lost in World War I were initially accepted by the Allies, and a policy known as appeasement was developed, which granted a series of concessions to Hitler in hope of preventing another war. However, by 1939, the Allied policy of appeasement had granted Germany so much land that Poland was surrounded on three sides

EUROPEAN COUNTRIES TODAY: POLAND

ABOVE: *The Nazi concentration camp at Auschwitz in Oświęcim.*

by Nazi possessions. When Poland refused Nazi proposals to join the Axis powers, Germany responded by invading Poland on September 1, 1939.

Polish forces were severely outnumbered and had no equipment to resist the state-of-the-art military technology employed by Germany.

Civilians suffered as Nazi planes bombed urban centers to weaken morale. In the end, despite fierce resistance, the Nazis overtook Poland.

Poland suffered greatly under Nazi rule. Not only were Polish Jews marked for extermination, as they were throughout Nazi-controlled Europe, but ethnic Poles were persecuted as well. Nearly one million Poles were deported to work in forced labor camps in Germany. Measures were taken to wipe out Polish culture and intellectual life. All universities and colleges were closed, and any Pole considered an "intellectual" was subject to execution. All education for Polish children beyond the primary level was banned. Poles were also

THE GOVERNMENT & HISTORY OF POLAND

Oskar Schindler and the Schindler Jews

German, Catholic, wealthy—all words that describe Oskar Schindler. There was little in his background to hint that he would play such an integral role in the survival of thousands of Jews in World War II Poland. After Germany invaded Poland, Schindler moved there to open a factory. To increase his profits, Schindler hired Jewish workers. German occupation meant that most of them had lost their prewar jobs. Desperate, they were the cheapest labor source Schindler could find. Schindler's accountant convinced some Jews who still had some wealth to invest in Schindler's factory. In return, they would be given a job and therefore less likely to be taken to concentration camps. Schindler treated his employees well.

After watching a 1942 German raid on the Jewish ghetto in Kraków, Schindler increased his attempts to help the Jewish population. He set up a "branch" of the Płaszów concentration camp in his Zabłocie factory compound and compiled a list of the people he would need to run it—Schindler's List. The factory lasted for more than a year making defective bullets for the German army. Two years later, Schindler moved the factory—and most of his employees—to Brunlitz.

Schindler escaped to Argentina with his wife and some employees after the war. Business venture after business venture failed, and Schindler left his family and returned to Germany in 1958. He spent the remaining years of his life traveling between Germany and Jerusalem.

During the last years of his life, Schindler was reportedly supported by those he called his *Schindlerjuden*—his children. The Israeli government honored him as one of the Righteous Among th eNations, the highest honor given to non-Jews who risked their lives to save Jews during the Holocaust. After his death in Germany in 1974, his body was taken to Jerusalem for burial on Mount Zion in Jerusalem. He had told a friend that he wanted to be buried in Jerusalem—where his children were.

Today, there are more Jews alive worldwide who owe their lives to Oskar Schindler than remain in Poland.

EUROPEAN COUNTRIES TODAY: POLAND

conscripted for forced labor in Poland itself, and several labor camps were scattered across the country. All told, the Nazis killed approximately three million Polish Jews. An additional three million non-Jewish Poles were also killed, or died as a result of Nazi occupation. In total, Poland lost more than 22 percent of its total population.

In June 1941, Hitler reneged on a nonaggression pact with the Soviets and invaded the Soviet Union. At war with the Soviets in the east and the Allies in the west, Hitler was outmatched. The Soviets marched across Poland in late 1944, and the German government there collapsed. A valiant attempt by Polish resistance forces to liberate Warsaw before the Soviet advance was brutally put down by the Nazis, and, by the time the Soviets arrived, Poland was unequipped for any further resistance. As Poland's boundaries were redrawn following World War II, the nation regained much of its hereditary lands, but it was now a Communist satellite state of the Soviet Union.

ABOVE: *Front page of the US Armed Forces newspaper,* The Stars and Stripes, *dated May 2, 1945, announcing Hitler's death.*

Communist Rule

In the years following World War II, Poland suffered under Communist rule. The country was in an economic shambles, and an entire generation of Poles were poorly educated, since they had not been allowed to attend school under Nazi occupation.

Various groups made several attempts to rebel against the Soviet-controlled Communist regime, but these were put down harshly. Because of its strategic location, Poland was a critical holding for the Soviets, so dissent could not be

THE GOVERNMENT & HISTORY OF POLAND

ABOVE: *The Palace of Culture and Science is a Warsaw landmark. This style of architecture is a legacy from the Communist era.*

EUROPEAN COUNTRIES TODAY: POLAND

tolerated. By the 1970s, an attempt at liberalizing the economy had failed, and the country faced a crisis as the nation's debt spiraled out of control and even the most basic consumer goods grew prohibitively expensive.

By 1980, a group of anti-Communist dissidents formed the independent trade union "Solidarity." Led by a shipyard electrician, Lech Wałęsa, the group promoted nonviolent protest as a means of political change and drew support from a wide variety of groups, including the Roman Catholic Church, academics, as well as laborers and farmers. Solidarity eventually became the leading force for resistance against Communism. By 1981, the Communists had outlawed Solidarity and imprisoned many of its leaders, which only served to gain the group even more popular support. The group continued to operate as an underground resistance movement, and, by 1988, it had gained enough strength that the Communist government began to negotiate openly with the organization. In 1990, the secretary general of the Communist Party resigned and was replaced by a coalition government led by Solidarity. In December of that year, Lech Wałęsa became the first popularly elected president of Poland.

ABOVE: Lech Wałęsa leader of "Solidarity," a resistance movement against Communism. He went on to become president (1990–95).

The Poland of Today

In the years since the fall of Communism, Poland has begun to emerge from centuries of foreign domination and economic hardship as a thriving democracy. Looking back to the days of the Nobles' Commonwealth, the Polish people feel they have a heritage of democracy and civil liberty and are working

THE GOVERNMENT & HISTORY OF POLAND

Karol Wojtyła

Who? He's perhaps better known as Pope John Paul II.

Karol Wojtyła was born in Wadowice, Poland, near Kraków, in 1920.

The future pope suffered much sadness in his childhood: his mother died when he was nine, and an older brother died when Karol was twelve. He himself was almost killed twice, first when struck by a streetcar and again when a truck hit him, which the athletic young man was able to overcome. In 1941, his father died, leaving Karol basically without a family.

In 1946, Karol Wojtyła was ordained a Catholic priest and served a church in Poland. After the Communists invaded Poland and ordered no church services to take place, Wojtyła defied the edict and offered worship services. After becoming pope in October 1978, this first non-Italian pope continued his fight against Communism. To many, Pope John Paul II was directly responsible for the fall of Communism worldwide.

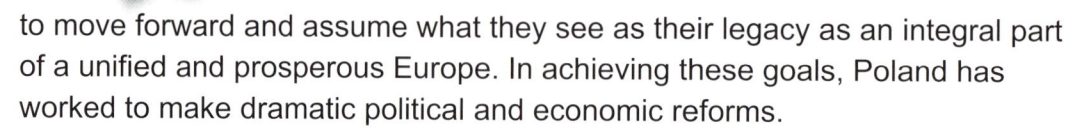

to move forward and assume what they see as their legacy as an integral part of a unified and prosperous Europe. In achieving these goals, Poland has worked to make dramatic political and economic reforms.

They are also seeking to enhance their prominence in international affairs.

EUROPEAN COUNTRIES TODAY: POLAND

Poland joined NATO in 1999 and became a member of the EU on May 1, 2004. These actions had widespread effects on the nation of Poland, particularly its economy. Today, Poland boasts the largest economy in Central Europe, and the eleventh largest in Europe. It is also the largest ex-Communist member of the European Union. Poland's transformation to a democratic, market-oriented country, with EU membership, has brought its economy and its politics up to date, so that today Poland is now considered to be an advanced Western country. It has made large investments in defense, energy, and other infrastructure, allowing it independence and autonomy.

As Poland is a member state that forms part of the EU's external border, it has had to implement the strict Schengen border rules to restrict illegal immigration and trade along its eastern borders with Belarus and Ukraine.

Text-Dependent Questions

1. Why was the Jagiellonian dynasty successful?

2. Who did Gavrilo Princip assassinate?

3. How many Polish Jews were killed by the Nazis?

Research Project

Write a biography on Lech Wałęsa.

THE GOVERNMENT & HISTORY OF POLAND

The Formation of the European Union (EU)

The EU is a confederation of European nations that continues to grow. As of 2017, there are twenty-eight official members. Several other candidates are also waiting for approval. All countries that enter the EU agree to follow common laws about foreign security policies. They also agree to cooperate on legal matters that go on within the EU. The European Council meets to discuss all international matters and make decisions about them. Each country's own concerns and interests are important, though. And apart from legal and financial issues, the EU tries to uphold values such as peace, human dignity, freedom, and equality.

All member countries remain autonomous. This means that they generally keep their own laws and regulations. The idea for a union among European nations was first mentioned after World War II. The war had devastated much of Europe, both physically and financially. In 1950, the French foreign minister suggested that France and West Germany combine their coal and steel industries under one authority. Both countries would have control over the

ABOVE: *The entrance to the European Union Parliament Building in Brussels.*

EUROPEAN COUNTRIES TODAY: POLAND

Member Countries

Austria	Greece	Romania
Belgium	Hungary	Slovakia
Bulgaria	Ireland	Slovenia
Croatia	Italy	Spain
Cyprus	Latvia	Sweden
Czech Republic	Lithuania	United Kingdom
Denmark	Luxembourg	*(Brexit: For the time*
Estonia	Malta	*being, the United*
Finland	Netherlands	*Kingdom remains a full*
France	Poland	*member of the EU.)*
Germany	Portugal	

industries. This would help them become more financially stable. It would also make war between the countries much more difficult. The idea was interesting to other European countries as well. In 1951, France, West Germany, Belgium, Luxembourg, the Netherlands, and Italy signed the Treaty of Paris, creating the European Coal and Steel Community. These six countries would become the core of the EU.

In 1957, these same countries signed the Treaties of Rome, creating the European Economic Community. In 1965, the Merger Treaty formed the European Community. Finally, in 1992, the Maastricht Treaty was signed. This treaty defined the European Union. It gave a framework for expanding the EU's political role, particularly in the area of foreign and security policy. It would also replace national currencies with the euro. The next year, the treaty went into effect. At that time, the member countries included the original six plus another six who had joined during the 1970s and '80s.

In the following years, the EU would take more steps to form a single market for its members. This would make joining the union even more advantageous. In addition to enlargement, the EU is steadily becoming more integrated through its own policies for closer cooperation between member states.

Words to Understand

Communist: Someone who supports a system of social organization in which all economic and social activity is controlled by the state, which is dominated by a single and self-perpetuating political party.

state ownership: A situation where property is owned by the state rather than individuals.

recession: A period of reduced economic activity.

BELOW: The Gdańsk Shipyard (Stocznia Gdańska) is a large shipyard located in the city of Gdańsk, on the Baltic Sea. The yard gained considerable fame because it was here, in 1980, that the independent trade union, Solidarity (Solidarność) was founded.

Chapter Three
THE POLISH ECONOMY

Poland is quickly moving from a period of economic hardship and **recession** to having the potential to be a major player on the world economic stage. With forty million consumers, Poland is the largest market in Central Europe, larger than the markets offered by the Czech Republic, Slovakia, and Hungary combined. The Polish economy also boasts one of the most impressive growth rates in the world. In the last few years, Poland is the only EU member nation to maintain growth of the country's gross domestic product (GDP) through the financial crisis that began in 2008.

ABOVE: *A liquid natural gas terminal at Świnoujście.*

THE POLISH ECONOMY

ABOVE: *Modern farming in Otmuchów.*

EUROPEAN COUNTRIES TODAY: POLAND

The New Economy
As Poland emerged from decades of **Communist** control, the economy was in a shambles. Large balances of unpaid foreign debt made borrowing difficult. And yet funds were needed to improve Poland's aged infrastructure before the nation could expect to see any real growth in foreign investment.

Privatization of industry and agriculture had begun before the collapse of the Communist government; however, major reforms were needed to return to the private ownership of businesses and to shift to a market economy after many years of **state ownership**. The new government instituted a program of "shock therapy" to revitalize the economy, and the dramatic reforms have paid off. Poland now has one of the most robust economies in all of Europe.

Industry: A Mainstay of the Economy and Exports
While not as large as it once was, heavy industry is an important part of Poland's economy. The services sector has grown in Poland in recent years, but manufacturing remains a major source of the nation's exports. The largest elements of the manufacturing sector are the automobile industry, iron and steel production, ship building, arms and weapons manufacture, and the chemical industry.

The increased demand for Polish products has enabled the Poles to rapidly develop a more modern infrastructure and dramatically increase productivity. The success of these industries has been essential to the country's economic recovery.

One of the fastest-growing branches of Poland's manufacturing sector is the defense industry. As a member of NATO, and as a border state of the EU, Poland has important military obligations that require a well-equipped, modern fighting force. Military electronics, such as targeting systems, explosives, and high-quality radar devices (produced by a company called Radwar), account for a large part of Poland's arms industry. In addition, the manufacture of heavy equipment, aircraft, and weaponry is expanding, and Poland has supply contracts all over the world.

The history of Poland's automotive industry goes back to the early 1930s, when the first Fiat plant was built in Poland. Today, Fiat is still the largest

45

THE POLISH ECONOMY

automaker to do business in Poland, but General Motors has also invested heavily in the country. Volkswagen and Toyota have parts assembly plants in there as well.

The Polish chemical industry is also thriving. Basic chemical products such as fertilizers, plastics, and dyes are produced by a number of Polish firms. The growth of the motor vehicle industry and the construction industry caused tremendous expansion in rubber manufacture, as demand for tires, treads for construction and military equipment, and PVC products rose accordingly.

Agriculture

Farming is a smaller but growing sector of the Polish economy. Poland is one of the world's largest producers of potatoes and rye. Other important food products produced and exported by Poland include pork, dairy products, poultry, and fruit. As conditions in Poland have improved, much of the food produced there now meets the high standards required for food to be exported to other EU nations. In addition, Polish farmers are counting on financial assistance from the EU to help build a more competitive agricultural industry. Agriculture is heavily subsidized by the EU's Common Agricultural Policy.

Educational Video

Poland pushes hard to become Eastern Europe's technology hub.

EUROPEAN COUNTRIES TODAY: POLAND

ABOVE: *Poland is one of the largest producers of potatoes in the world.*

THE POLISH ECONOMY

Energy Sources and Transportation

Poland is committed to implementing all aspects of the EU's energy policy. Environmental protection and conservation are among the most important factors of Poland's new energy policy, and it is critical to Poland's interests that the country develops new sources of energy to guarantee its future energy security. In addition to researching new and renewable energy sources, changes have been made in the way Poland uses its current energy sources. New natural gas pipelines have been built, linking Poland with Norway and Germany. Poland's electrical system was joined with the Western European grid in the early 2000s, making it possible for Poland to sell its excess electrical power. Coal still remains the largest source of energy in Poland, but new advances have made this dependence on coal less damaging to the

ABOVE: *A modern factory in Szczecin that produces components for wind farms.*

EUROPEAN COUNTRIES TODAY: POLAND

The Economy of Poland

Gross Domestic Product (GDP): $1 trillion (2016 est.)
GDP Per Capita: $27,700 (2016 est.)
Industries: machine building, iron and steel, coal mining, chemicals, shipbuilding, food processing, glass, beverages, textiles
Agriculture: potatoes, fruits, vegetables, wheat; poultry, eggs, pork, dairy
Export Commodities: machinery and transport equipment 37.8%, intermediate manufactured goods 23.7%, miscellaneous manufactured goods 17.1%, food and live animals 7.6%
Export Partners: Germany 27.3%, UK 6.6%, Czech Republic 6.6%, France 5.4%, Italy 4.8%, Netherlands 4.5% (2016)
Import Commodities: machinery and transport equipment 38%, intermediate manufactured goods 21%, chemicals 15%, minerals, fuels, lubricants, and related materials 9%
Import Partners: Germany 28.3%, China 7.9%, Netherlands 6%, Russia 5.8%, Italy 5.3%, France 4.2%, Czech Republic 4.1% (2016)
Currency: złoty

Source: www.cia.gov 2017

environment and more efficient. New sources of power, such as geothermal energy and wind and solar power, are slowly reducing the large portion of Poland's energy provided by coal.

Transportation

Highways, railways, waterways (both navigable rivers and canals located on modern ports and harbors), and airports make up Poland's complex

THE POLISH ECONOMY

ABOVE: A container ship is being loaded at the Deepwater Container Terminal at Gdańsk.

transportation system. Five international airports connect Poland with the rest of the world, and Warsaw is quickly becoming the main transportation center for all of Central Europe. Poland's seaports are also vital transport centers, not only for Poland but for many of the landlocked nations of Central Europe as well. Polish ports are currently undergoing a period of restructuring to integrate shipping more smoothly with Poland's highways, railways, and air transport systems.

EUROPEAN COUNTRIES TODAY: POLAND

Poland's Economy Today

Even though Poland has achieved great success since the fall of Communism, it still has many systemic challenges to face in the twenty-first century. Poland's road and rail infrastructure are not sufficiently modernized to support an optimum business environment and the country still has to contend with a rigid labor code, government red tape, and a burdensome tax system left over from the Communist era. Additional long-term challenges include modernizing and diversifying Poland's energy supplies and securing investment for industry, research, and development. The country has also had to contend with the the outflow of educated young Poles to other EU member states and a low birth rate. However, despite these challenges, recent figures from the World Bank have classifed Poland as a high-income economy and ranked it twenty-third worldwide in terms of GDP. In 2017, the Polish market was upgraded from an emerging market to developed status.

Text-Dependent Questions

1. What was the state of Poland's economy after the fall of Communism?

2. Name some important Polish exports.

3. Why are Poland's seaports important to other European countries?

Research Project

Write a brief report on Poland's automobile industry.

Words to Understand

homogeneous: Of the same or similar kind or nature.

vernacular: The language or dialect that is most commonly spoken by ordinary people in a region or country.

vocational: Relating to training in a skill or trade to be pursued as a career.

BELOW: Toruń, in northern Poland, is a very old city, having been established in 1233 by the Teutonic Knights. At one time, the city was considered the most modern cultural and technological center in medieval Europe. Interestingly, Toruń was the birthplace of astronomer Nicolaus Copernicus.

Chapter Four
CITIZENS OF POLAND: PEOPLE, CUSTOMS & CULTURE

Poland, home to nearly forty million people, is the largest country in Central Europe. The nation is ethnically **homogeneous**, with more than 97 percent of the population identifying themselves as Polish. The country is also almost 90 percent Roman Catholic, although only about 75 percent of those who identify as Catholic actively practice their faith. Although other religious faiths in Poland are small in number, Polish worshippers today have complete freedom of religion. The Poles also have a strong national identity and are proud of their rich heritage and culture.

Education and Sports: An Educated and Active People

Poland is a nation that takes education very seriously. The literacy rate for adults is very high, and many Poles can converse in another language. The country has produced famous thinkers and athletes.

In Poland, education is compulsory, and every child between ages seven and sixteen must attend school. The school system, though, is quite different from that in North America. To begin, all children attend *Szkoła podstawowa* for six years. Next, students attend the *Gimnazjum*, or secondary school, for three years, after which they must complete a comprehensive exam. Depending on the student's interests and grades, there are several different options after completing Gimnazjum; each young person's path depends on whether he or she is interested in **vocational** training or pursuing study at the university level.

When it comes to sports, Poles don't believe in just sitting on the sidelines. They go out and play themselves. Community centers offer sports complexes, pools, and athletic leagues for the public. Many different sporting events are held in Poland each year, although soccer is by far the most popular sport. If an important soccer match is being broadcast on television, the city streets may be deserted. Poland's most famous athlete is retired Adam Małysz, a world-

CITIZENS OF POLAND: PEOPLE, CUSTOMS & CULTURE

ABOVE: *World-famous ski jumper champion, Adam Małysz, is now retired.*

champion ski jumper. Poland also boasts a proud Olympic history, with many Polish athletes winning medals over the years. Tennis, hockey, cycling, canoeing, sailing, swimming, skiing, and hiking are other popular sports.

EUROPEAN COUNTRIES TODAY: POLAND

Educational Video

A video about sports in Poland and some famous sportsmen and women.

ABOVE: *Students in an IT lesson at a school in Bolesławiec.*

CITIZENS OF POLAND: PEOPLE, CUSTOMS & CULTURE

Food and Drink

Proud of their hearty appetites, Poles have traditionally preferred simple, meat-and-potatoes-style fare. Western influences in Poland today have brought some changes in eating habits. In Poland's urban centers, people enjoy foreign foods such as pizza, pasta, and even Chinese and Mexican cuisine. For most Poles, however, the traditional favorites dominate. Meat, stews, potatoes, and cabbage are the staples of Polish cuisine. As in much of Central Europe, beer and wine are popular beverages. A variety of fruit-flavored liquors and vodka are also available.

ABOVE: *Stews made with meat and vegetables are traditionally eaten in Poland.*

EUROPEAN COUNTRIES TODAY: POLAND

Klopsiki w Śmietanie
(Polish Meatballs)

Makes about 6 servings

Ingredients
1 kaiser roll
½ cup milk
1 pound ground beef
¼ pound ground pork
1 egg
1 small onion, grated
2–3 tablespoons oil
¼ cup sour cream
2 tablespoons flour
dill, chopped
salt and pepper to taste

Directions
Let kaiser roll sit overnight, until it is hard. Soak roll in ½ cup of milk until mixture is soggy. Mash with fork. Combine ground meat, raw egg, and onion with bread mixture. Mix all ingredients well, and add salt and pepper to taste. Roll into golf-ball-sized meatballs. In a frying pan coated with oil, brown the meatballs on all sides. Transfer browned meatballs to a baking pan, add 2 tablespoons of water, and bake at 325° F for 30 minutes. Remove pan from the oven and drain drippings. Mix pan drippings with flour and sour cream. Pour mixture back over the meatballs and bake for five more minutes. Garnish with freshly chopped dill. For a traditional Polish dinner, serve with mashed potatoes and beets.

Mizeria (Cucumber Salad)

Ingredients
3 large cucumbers, chilled
salt and pepper to taste
1 teaspoon sugar
1 teaspoon lemon juice
¾ cup sour cream
dill and unpeeled cucumber slices for a garnish

Directions
Peel and thinly slice cucumber. Sprinkle with salt, pepper, and sugar. Toss lightly with lemon juice until the cucumber is evenly coated. Add sour cream and mix. Garnish with the unpeeled cucumber and a sprig of dill.

CITIZENS OF POLAND: PEOPLE, CUSTOMS & CULTURE

Music and Literature

Literary works written in the Polish **vernacular** date back to before the fourteenth century. In the centuries that followed, Polish literature flourished, much of it in the form of poetry. Examples of important Polish literature can be found in almost all the famous literary styles that occurred in Europe, notably Renaissance, baroque, and neoclassicist works.

Poland's great heyday of Romanticist literature occurred in the nineteenth century and inspired the nationalist ambitions of the Polish people. Henryk Sienkiewicz won the Nobel Prize for Literature for his book *Quo Vadis*, written in 1905. In the turmoil of the twentieth century, many Polish writers continued to publish important works in exile, having fled the destruction of the world wars or the oppression of the Communist regime. Another Nobel Prize winner, Czesław Miłosz, was one of these émigré writers.

In music, Poles have made important contributions as well. The romanticism that gripped nineteenth-century Poland inspired the music of Frédéric Chopin, which is now among the best-loved classical music of all time. Chopin in turn stimulated the nationalist aspirations of his fellow Poles by introducing elements of tradtional Polish folk music into his works. The same period produced the growth of the Polish opera, with Stanisław Moniuszko as its most recognized composer.

ABOVE: *Henryk Sienkiewicz.*

ABOVE: *Stanisław Moniuszko.*

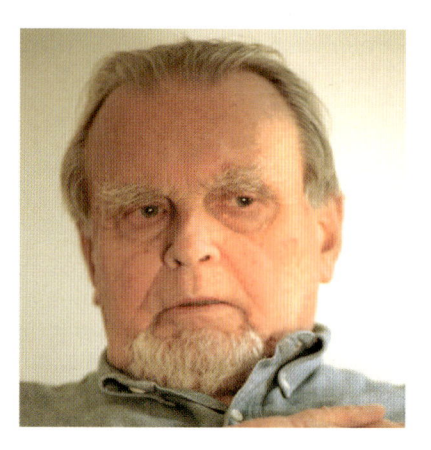

ABOVE: *Czesław Miłosz.*

EUROPEAN COUNTRIES TODAY: POLAND

Folk music still occupies a prominent place in Polish culture. People around the world recognize traditional Polish dance music such as the polka and the mazurka. Today, tourists and locals alike frequent the many cultural festivals that highlight Polish music and dancing.

Modern music also has a prominent place in today's Poland. The country has always been very open to new styles of music, and, even before the fall of Communism, Western popular music had gained an audience in Poland. While pop music is common, its popularity is surpassed by the Polish love of hard rock and hip-hop styles of music. Many Polish artists are producing their own varieties of hip-hop and rock music. Polish jazz also has a small but dedicated following. Jazz festivals feature this blend of a uniquely American musical style fused with compositions characteristically Polish in flavor.

ABOVE: *Polish folk dancers in Kraków's main square celebrating Poland's Constitution Day, which is a national holiday.*

CITIZENS OF POLAND: PEOPLE, CUSTOMS & CULTURE

Arts and Architecture

Traditionally, Poland has been a land of grand architecture. History has not been kind to many of Poland's architectural treasures, however. In particular, the devastation caused by the two world wars destroyed many fine monuments and buildings of historic and artistic significance.

Nonetheless, some of Poland's most important architecture has survived or been painstakingly rebuilt or restored. Many of the best examples can be seen in Kraków, where many important Gothic and Renaissance structures have been preserved. The town of Kazimierz Dolny, on the banks of the Wisła River, is one of the best-preserved medieval towns in Europe.

Marie Curie

Poles are not just famous for artistic, musical, and literary achievements. Marie Skłodowska Curie, the first person to win or share two Nobel Prizes, was born in Warsaw, Poland, in 1867.

After graduating from high school, she was unable to study at any Russian or Polish universities because she was female. So Marie worked as a governess for several years. Eventually, with financial assistance from an older sister, Marie was able to attend the Sorbonne, in Paris, where she studied chemistry and physics. It was there that she met her husband, Pierre Curie, and, together, they studied radioactive materials, discovering radium and polonium.

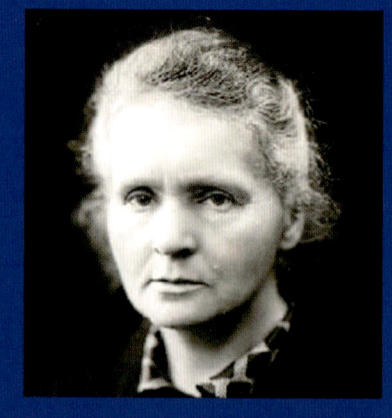

Curie died from leukemia in 1934, most likely caused by her long-term exposure to radiation in her work. A year after her death, her eldest daughter won the Noble Prize for Chemistry.

EUROPEAN COUNTRIES TODAY: POLAND

ABOVE: *The town of Kazimierz Dolny, on the Wisła River, is famous for its artists and art galleries.*

Malbork Castle, Malbork

The Polish town of Malbork was formerly in East Prussia, and better known historically by its German name, Marienburg. The castle was built for the Teutonic Knights, and was their headquarters for over a century.

The castle was built on the site of an earlier structure on a hill near the River Nogat. As the headquarters of the Grand Master of the Teutonic Knights in the fourteenth century, it became one of the largest and most powerful castles in Germany. It was built of brick, with steepish red-tile roofs and turrets in a recognizably "Baltic" style, seen also in the cities originally responsible for the founding of the Order. The Grand Master ruled his Baltic empire in some style, and great banquets were held under the immensely high vault of the great hall. This is one of the most impressive buildings of the old castle, along with the chapel. This was, after all, the home of a religious order, and the knights never entirely forgot their religious responsibilities.

The castle's heyday was short. The defeat of the knights by the king of Poland at Tannenberg in 1410 marked the beginning of their decline.

CITIZENS OF POLAND: PEOPLE, CUSTOMS & CULTURE

ABOVE: Jan Matejko, Self-portrait, *1892.*

EUROPEAN COUNTRIES TODAY: POLAND

Poles are proud of their contributions to the visual arts as well. Perhaps the most famous contribution to the visual arts was Jan Matejko's illustrious school of Historicist painting. These paintings, inspired by the Romanticism and nationalist pride of the nineteenth century, portrayed important events from Poland's history on a monumental scale. In addition to painting, Poles have made significant contributions in the fields of sculpture, photography, and cinema.

Text-Dependent Questions

1. What is a *Skoła podstawowa*?

2. Which prize did Henryk Sienkiewicz win?

3. What is the German name for the town of Malbork?

Research Project

Find a Polish recipe other than the ones given in this chapter, and ask an adult to help you make it. Share it with members of your class.

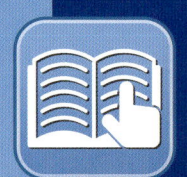

Words to Understand

botanical: Relating to plants or botany.

coexist: To live in peace with each other.

metropolis: A large, important city.

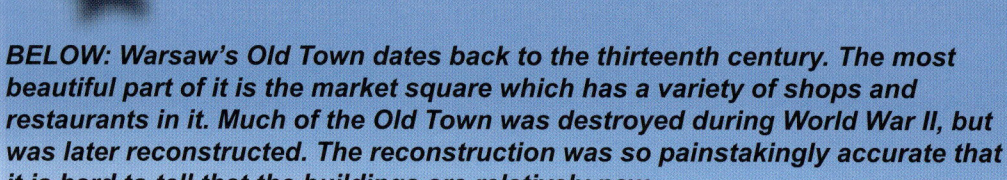

BELOW: Warsaw's Old Town dates back to the thirteenth century. The most beautiful part of it is the market square which has a variety of shops and restaurants in it. Much of the Old Town was destroyed during World War II, but was later reconstructed. The reconstruction was so painstakingly accurate that it is hard to tell that the buildings are relatively new.

Chapter Five
THE FAMOUS CITIES OF POLAND

Today's Poland is an urban society. Much of the population live in cities and towns, and the standard of living has improved with the economic growth that followed the collapse of the Communist government. Modern Polish families tend to be quite small; couples usually have only one child, and many have none.

Most of Poland's cities are medium-sized or small; only a few large cities exist. Most Polish cities are centuries old and built upon ancient trade routes and waterways. Today, modern structures **coexist** with ancient monuments, Gothic churches, and Soviet-era factories and apartment complexes.

Polish cities also consciously promote a rich cultural life. Many towns subsidize theaters, music festivals, and art exhibits.

Varied Population Density

Poland is comprised of sixteen provinces, whose population densities vary greatly. The most densely populated are those that

ABOVE: A detail of the Warsaw Uprising Monument. It is a tribute to the Polish insurgents who fought against Nazi occupation in 1944.

THE FAMOUS CITIES OF POLAND

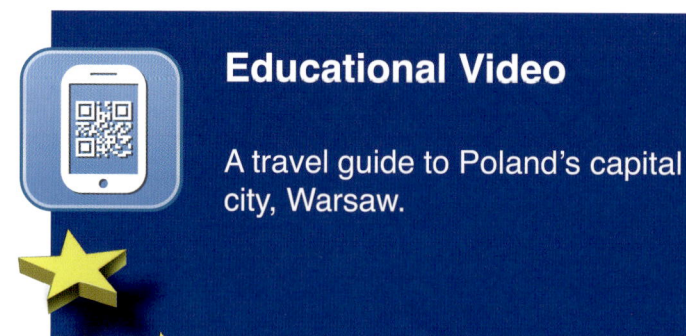

Educational Video

A travel guide to Poland's capital city, Warsaw.

ABOVE: *The neomodern Q22 tower is the fourth-tallest building in Poland.*

EUROPEAN COUNTRIES TODAY: POLAND

ABOVE: *The Warsaw Barbican is one of the few remaining relics of the complex network of historic fortifications that once encircled Warsaw.*

include major urban centers like Warsaw, Łódź, and Kraków. Agricultural areas are the least populated, with many families working their own small farms in rural communities.

Warsaw: The Capital

Warsaw, located on the Wisła River, near the center of the country, is Poland's capital and most populated city. The city is home to many important industries, sixty-six different colleges and universities, and more than thirty different theater companies, including the National Theater and Opera and the Philharmonic National Orchestra. Warsaw is perhaps most remarkable for the

69

THE FAMOUS CITIES OF POLAND

ABOVE: The Royal Castle in Warsaw was burned and looted by the Nazis following the invasion of Poland in 1939. It was almost completely destroyed in 1944 after the failed Warsaw Uprising. The castle was completely rebuilt in 1965.

EUROPEAN COUNTRIES TODAY: POLAND

fact that it has survived for so long. The city suffered assaults in 1655 and 1794. It was then severely bombed during the German invasion of Poland in World War II, and after the retreat of German troops in 1944 Hitler ordered the entire city to be destroyed. Eighty-five percent of the city was completely flattened. Nevertheless, the city continued as Poland's capital, and today Warsaw is the center of Polish political, economic, and cultural life. Many of the old structures have been rebuilt, and the historic Old Town of Warsaw is on the World Heritage List.

ABOVE: *The classical Łazienki Palace is situated in Warsaw's Royal Baths Park, which is the city's largest park.*

THE FAMOUS CITIES OF POLAND

ABOVE: *Piotrkowska Street in Łódź is the town's main shopping street.*

Łódź

Poland's second-most populated city, Łódź, is home to many of Poland's most important industries. The city is now a thriving **metropolis**, boasting not only a number of important industries but several parks, a zoo, **botanical** gardens, and one of Poland's best-known art museums. The city is also home to a number of important eighteenth- and nineteenth-century structures. The University of Łódź and the Technical University of Łódź draw in students from all over Poland.

EUROPEAN COUNTRIES TODAY: POLAND

Manufaktura

The Manufaktura complex in Łódź is a center for the arts and a venue for international concerts. It is also shopping mall with restaurants and bars.

The complex is home to the largest public square in Łódź, which is now a major tourist attraction. The Manufaktura opened in May 2006, after nine years of planning and construction. The total area of the complex is a staggering 67 acres (27 hectares). The work involved the restoration of factory buildings previously used by the textile industry. The original ninteenth-century brick buildings remain the most interesting part of the complex, having been restored brick by brick. The only missing elements are the chimney stacks that once dominated the skyline.

Wawel Castle, Kraków

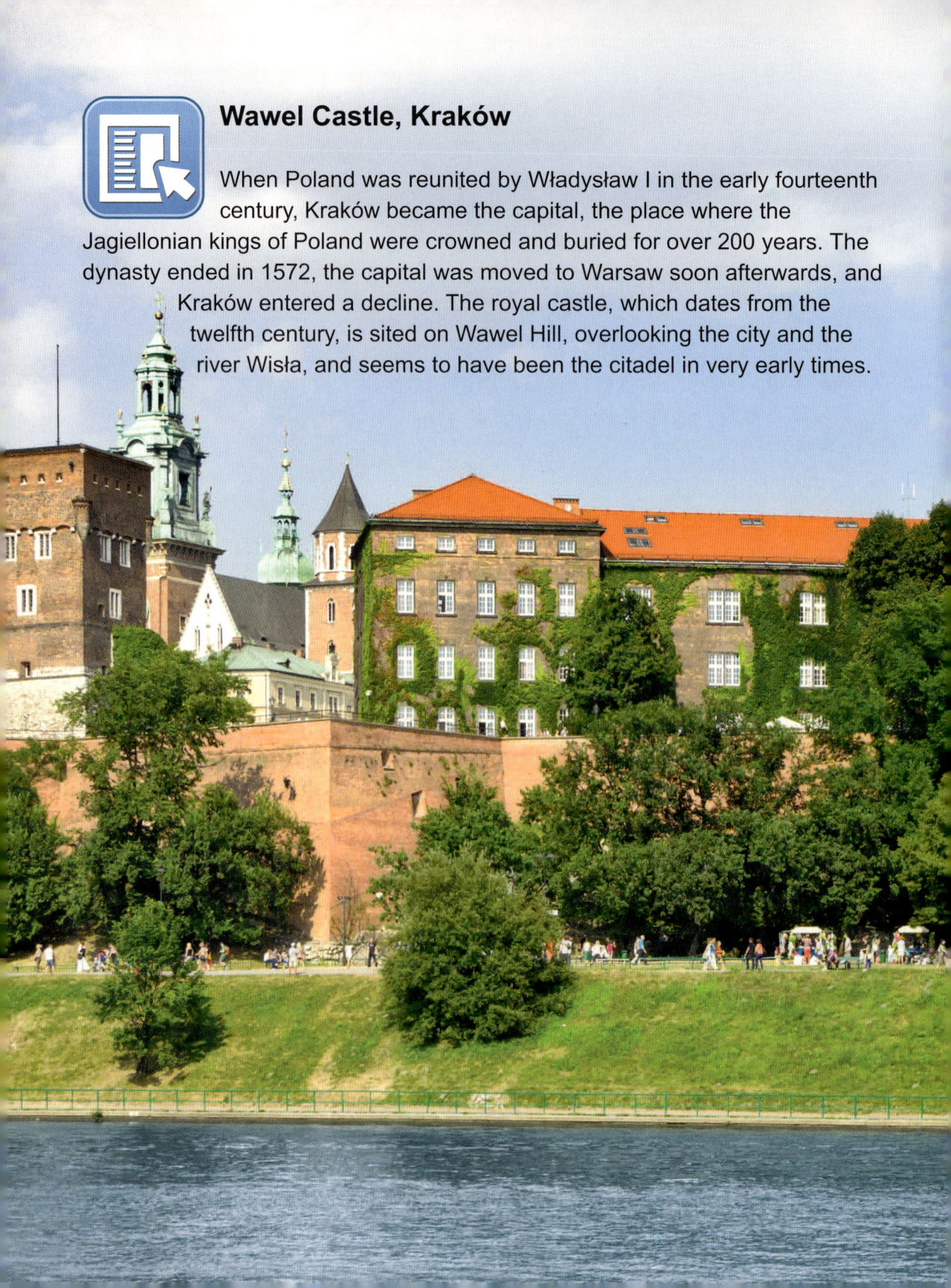

When Poland was reunited by Władysław I in the early fourteenth century, Kraków became the capital, the place where the Jagiellonian kings of Poland were crowned and buried for over 200 years. The dynasty ended in 1572, the capital was moved to Warsaw soon afterwards, and Kraków entered a decline. The royal castle, which dates from the twelfth century, is sited on Wawel Hill, overlooking the city and the river Wisła, and seems to have been the citadel in very early times.

Essentially, the building is a Polish medieval castle that between 1507 and 1536 was turned into an Italian Renaissance palace by craftsmen imported from Italy. This gave rise to some odd conjunctions, such as the little tent-like pavilion that rests on a convenient Gothic battlement, but the overall effect is quite harmonious.

The large and impressive central courtyard is surrounded by distinctive three-tiered arcades. Interestingly, one of the four blocks surrounding the courtyard is a dummy. There are no habitable rooms behind its façade; it was built for the sake of symmetry alone.

THE FAMOUS CITIES OF POLAND

ABOVE: *St. Mary's Basilica is next to the main market square in Kraków. It was built in the fourteenth century, although its foundations date back to the early thirteenth century. It is considered one of the best examples of Polish Gothic architecture.*

EUROPEAN COUNTRIES TODAY: POLAND

Kraków

Situated in the south of Poland, Kraków, once the nation's capital, is the nation's third-largest city. Settlement of Kraków dates back to the fourth century, and the city is now considered the cultural heart of Poland. It is home to Poland's oldest university, and today hosts eighteen different universities, colleges, and technical schools. The city also has twenty-eight museums, numerous concert halls, and theaters. Tourists are attracted to the city's rich architecture; structures can be found in Kraków representing Renaissance, baroque, and Gothic styles.

Kraków also hosts many important cultural events, such as the Festival of Short Feature Films, the Biennial of Graphics, and the Jewish Cultural Festival.

ABOVE: *The Jewish Quarter of the Kazimierz district in Kraków.*

THE FAMOUS CITIES OF POLAND

Poznań

Poznań is the fourth-largest industrial center in Poland. Located in the western part of the country on the Warta River, Poznań is a vital center for trade, industry, and education. Poznań also has historic significance: its cathedral is the earliest surviving church in Poland and contains the tombs of several early Polish rulers. Poznań is now the major center for trade with Germany and is home to a number of industries as well as important colleges and universities.

ABOVE: *St. Stanislaus Church in the old town of Poznań has some of the most beautiful baroque features in Poland. The church was completed around 1750.*

EUROPEAN COUNTRIES TODAY: POLAND

ABOVE: The old market square in Poznań is home to a magnificent Renaissance town hall. The building in its current form dates back to around 1560.

THE FAMOUS CITIES OF POLAND

Gdańsk

With a thriving shipbuilding industry, Gdańsk is Poland's primary seaport. It is a crucial transport center not only for Poland but for neighboring countries with no seaports of their own. In addition to shipping and shipbuilding, the port city is also home to a large share of Poland's chemical and electronic industries. Gdańsk has ten different colleges and universities and holds many important cultural events each year.

ABOVE: *Old town houses next to the Motława River in Gdańsk.*

EUROPEAN COUNTRIES TODAY: POLAND

ABOVE: A ship under construction at the Gdańsk shipyard.

Text-Dependent Questions

1. What river is Warsaw located on?

2. Where is the oldest university in Poland?

3. Where is Poland's main seaport?

Research Project

Write an essay on one of Poland's beautiful towns or cities not mentioned in this chapter and explain which features makes it so remarkable.

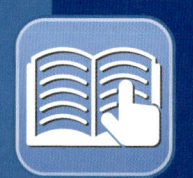

Words to Understand

equality: The state or quality of being equal.

poverty: The state or condition of having little or no money, goods, or means of support; the condition of being poor.

refugees: People who flee for refuge or safety, especially to a foreign country, as in times of political upheaval, war, etc.

BELOW: *A walker on a trail in the Tatra Mountains, which lie between Poland and Slovkia.*

Chapter Six
A BRIGHT FUTURE FOR POLAND

In many ways, Poland's future looks bright. This is a big change from Poland's twentieth-century image. Back then, many people connected Poland with **poverty**, suffering, **refugees**, and unrest. The nation had been fought over for centuries; it had been invaded, divided, and conquered. Its people had very little hope.

But all of that's different in the twenty-first century. Today, Poland is a thriving member of the EU—and, despite its ongoing problems, it is forging ahead toward the future with confidence and strength. Its relationships with its two larger neighbors, Germany and Russia, are now based on **equality** and respect. Many Polish immigrants who left their homeland in the twentieth century in search of better opportunities in the UK are now starting to return home.

As a member of the EU, Poland still has challenges to face in the future. One of the biggest of these has to do with its energy sources. The EU is committed to reducing its dependence on carbon-based fuels, and Poland is still dependent on coal for much of its fuel and

ABOVE: *Polish and EU flags.*

A BRIGHT FUTURE FOR POLAND

ABOVE: *Active coal mine in Dąbrowa Górnicza. Poland relies on coal for most of its electricity.*

electricity. Many Polish leaders want their nation to switch to natural gas, which would allow Poland to continue to be economically independent. But the EU is concerned that Poland's methods of extracting natural gas could further contribute to global climate change.

Until recently, Poland's leaders felt that, as a young nation, Poland needed to continue to develop its economy before it could focus on the environment. They believed that this would fast-track their country to a strong future. This approach, however, did draw criticism from other EU members, especially France. Polish politicians claimed their country should have the right to make its own energy decisions.

However, Poland is fortunate to own good renewable energy resources, with its high levels of exploitable wind power and good biogas potential. A study by the Global Wind Energy Council found that the country could potentially meet a large percentage of its energy needs with wind farms by 2020.

EUROPEAN COUNTRIES TODAY: POLAND

ABOVE: A thermal power station in Gdańsk.

A BRIGHT FUTURE FOR POLAND

The country has committed to getting 15 percent of its energy from renewable sources by 2020, and 20 percent by 2030. But many Polish officials insist that their land does not have strong enough winds to make the wind turbines work. These officials also claim that in "scenic rural areas, people don't want windmills because they say it will destroy the picturesque view." One Polish official told journalists that "windmills are not good for the birds and the animals living underground. They're also not good for fish, because [they make the] fish disappear. In fact this equipment also produces infrasound which we don't hear, but animals can." But a spokesperson for the European Wind Energy Association (EWEA) says these claims are nonsense; "Wind power is supported by all the major environmental groups," he said, "because it's a clean source of power which combats climate change, the greatest threat to biodiversity. Wind energy causes fewer bird fatalities than power lines, buildings or vehicles, and the EWEA has never come across instances of harm to underground animals or fish caused by wind turbines."

ABOVE: *A wind farm on farmland near the town of Otmuchów.*

EUROPEAN COUNTRIES TODAY: POLAND

What Is Global Climate Change—and Why Are People So Worried About It?

Global climate change has to do with an average increase in the Earth's temperature. Most scientists agree that humans are responsible because of the pollution cars and factories have put into the air.

Global warming is already having serious impacts on humans and the environment in many ways. An increase in global temperatures causes rising sea levels (because of melting of the polar caps) and changes in the amount and pattern of precipitation. These changes may increase the frequency and intensity of extreme weather events, such as floods, droughts, heat waves, hurricanes, and tornados. Other consequences include changes to farms' crop production, species becoming extinct, and an increased spread of disease.

Not all experts agree about climate change, but almost all scientists believe that it is very real. Politicians and the public do not agree, though, on policies to deal with climate change. Changes in the way people live can be expensive, at both the personal and national levels, and not everyone is convinced that taking on these expenses needs to be a priority.

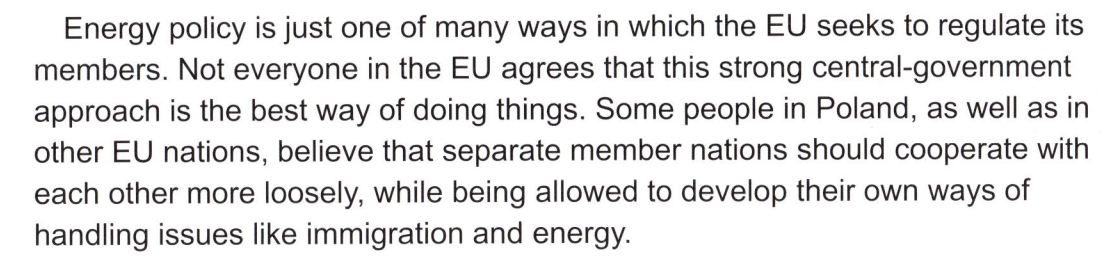

Energy policy is just one of many ways in which the EU seeks to regulate its members. Not everyone in the EU agrees that this strong central-government approach is the best way of doing things. Some people in Poland, as well as in other EU nations, believe that separate member nations should cooperate with each other more loosely, while being allowed to develop their own ways of handling issues like immigration and energy.

A BRIGHT FUTURE FOR POLAND

For the most part, however, Poland believes that its future lies firmly connected with the European Union. In July 2011, when Poland took on the six-month rotating presidency of the EU for the first time, Polish prime minister

ABOVE: Polish Prime Minister Mateusz Morawiecki was appointed prime minister in a ceremony in Warsaw on December 11, 2017.

EUROPEAN COUNTRIES TODAY: POLAND

Donald Tusk said that Poland is a "European success story," "a symbol of hope, optimism, energy, and strength." Europe has invested a lot in Poland's future, the prime minister added—and now Poland will invest its energy in Europe's future.

According to the McKinsey report, Poland's impressive history of growth for more than two decades has left the country poised to become a regional growth engine. Over the past twenty-five years, the Polish economy has doubled in size, as measured by real GDP.

The country now stands as an advanced European economy competing on a global stage. With its transformation from a communist to a democratic, market-oriented country, it is now a major player in international politics and an increasingly active member of Euro-Atlantic organizations.

Text-Dependent Questions

1. Why is the EU committed to reducing its dependence on carbon-based fuels?

2. How does Poland generate the majority of its electricity?

3. Why is wind power clean energy?

Research Project

Write a report on Poland's relationship with the EU and role in it.

CHRONOLOGY

966   Mieszko I receives the title of duke and is the first to institute central rule in Poland. Poland begins to convert to Roman Catholicism.
1025   The Kingdom of Poland is established.
1385   The Kingdom of Poland-Lithuania is created.
1795   Poland is divided up between by three different states in the last of three partitions.
1914   World War I begins.
1918   Poland is reestablished as an independent nation.
1939   Germany invades Poland, and World War II begins.
1945   Allies defeat Germany in World War II.
1945   Soviets institute a Communist government in Poland.
1951   The six countries that formed the core of the European Union sign the Treaty of Paris.
1980   Solidarity is formed.
1988   The Communist Party begins formal negotiations with Solidarity.
1990   The Communist secretary general resigns, and Lech Walesa is elected president.
1992   The Maastricht Treaty creates the EU.
1999   Poland joins NATO.
2003   Poles vote for membership in the EU.
2004   Poland officially joins the EU.
2008   Global recession begins.
2010   The Polish parliament declares August 2 to be the official Roma and Sinti Genocide Remembrance Day.
2011   Prime Minister Donald Tusk's center-right Civic Platform party wins parliamentary elections.
2015   Conservative Law and Justice candidate Andrzej Duda beats centrist incumbent Bronisław Komorowski in presidential election.
2017   Prime Minister Mateusz Morawiecki is appointed prime minister.
2017   Tens of thousands of people take part in a march in the capital, Warsaw, to protest against what they see as curbs on democracy imposed by the governing Law and Justice Party.

Further Reading

Baker, Mark. Di Luca, Mark. *Lonely Planet Poland (Travel Guide)*. London: Lonely Planet Publications, 2016.

McCormick, John. *Understanding the European Union: A Concise Introduction*. London: Palgrave Macmillan, 2017.

Mason, David S. *A Concise History of Modern Europe: Liberty, Equality, Solidarity.* London: Rowman & Littlefield, 2015.

Steves, Rick. Hewitt, Cameron. *Rick Steves' Snapshot Kraków, Warsaw & Gdansk.* Edmonds: Rick Steves' Europe, Inc. 2017.

Internet Resources

Poland Travel Information and Travel Guide
www.lonelyplanet.com/poland

Poland's Official Travel Website
https://www.poland.travel/en-gb

Poland: Country Profile
http://www.bbc.co.uk/news/world-europe-17753718

Poland: CIA World Factbook
https://www.cia.gov/library/publications/the-world-factbook/geos/pl.html

The Official Website of the European Union
europa.eu/index_en.htm

Publisher's note:
The websites listed on this page were active at the time of publication. The publisher is not responsible for websites that have changed their addresses or discontinued operation since the date of publication. The publisher will review and update the website list upon each reprint.

INDEX

A
AD (anno Domini), 24
Advancement, 38–39
Agriculture, 13, 44, 45, 46, 49, 69
Airports, 50
Allies, 32
Andrić, Ivo, 26
Animals, 16, 17–19
Anti-Communists, 8
Appeasement, 32–35
Architecture, 27, 60, 62–63, 77
    Polish Gothic, 76
Area, 7, 11
Argentina, 34
Arts, 27, 30, 61, 64, 64. 65, 65, 73
Auschwitz, 33
Austria, 28, 30
Axis Powers, 32–35, 33

B
Baltic
    Sea, 10, 11, 14, 17, 42
    style, 62
BC (Before Christ), 24
Belarus, 7, 11, 25, 39
Belgium, 30, 41
Belorussians, 27
Biennial of Graphics, 77
Birth rate, 9
Bolesław I Chrobry, 22, 23
Bolesławiec, 55
Bonaparte, Napoleon, 28
Borders, 7
Brunlitz, 34
Brussels, 40

C
Calvinists, 26
Capital, 11, 69
Carpathian Mountains, 12, 13, 14
Casimir III the Great, 26
CE (Common Era), 24
China, 49
Chopin, Frédéric, 58
Cities, 67–81
Climate, 7, 15
    change, 87
    continental, 15
Coal, 48, 83–84
Coastal plain, 11
Communist rule, 35, 37, 45
Concentration camp, 33
Constitution Day, 59
Copernicus, Nicolaus, 26, 27, 52
Crusades, 23
Cucumber salad, 57
Curie
    Marie, 60
    Pierre, 60
Currency, 41, 49
Czech
    people, 27
    Republic, 7, 11, 13, 49

D
Dąbrowa Górnicza, 84
Dance, 59
Dating systems, 24
David, Jacques Louis, 28
Death rate, 9
Deepwater Container Terminal, 50
Democracy, 27, 37, 39
Duchy of Warsaw, 30

E
East Prussia, 62
Economy, 39, 43–51, 49, 84, 89
    growth rates, 43
    new, 45
    today, 51
Education, 33, 53
    system, 53
Electricity, 48
Elevation, 7
Emigration, 51
Energy, 48–49, 83–86
    policy, 87
    renewable, 48, 84, 86
Ethnic groups, 9, 26–27
    conflicts among, 30
    homogenous, 53
Eurasian lynx, 17
Euro, 41
European
    bison, 19
    Coal and Steel Community, 41
    Council, 40
    Economic Community, 41
    honey buzzard, 18
    Wind Energy Association, 86
European Union (EU), 21, 39, 45, 46, 84, 87, 88
    autonomy, 40
    flag, 83
    formation, 40–41
    members, 40, 41
    Parliament Building, 40

INDEX

single market, 41
values, 40
Exports, 45, 49

F
Ferdinand, Archduke Franz, 30, 31
Fertility rate, 9
Festival of Short Feature Films, 77
Fiat, 45–46
Flag, 8, 83
Food and drink, 56–57
Forced labor, 35
  camps, 33, 34
France, 28, 30, 32–35, 40, 41, 49, 84
Freedom, 27
Future, 83–89

G
Gdańsk, 50, 80–81, 85
  Shipyard (Stocznia Gdańska), 42, 81
General Motors, 46
Geography, 7
  and landscape, 11–19
Geothermal power, 38
German people, 9, 23, 27
Germany, 7, 11, 21, 30, 49, 83
  invasion by, 33
Gimnazjum, 53
Global
  climate change, 87
  warming, 87
Global
  Wind Energy Council, 84
Golden age, 25–28

Goplans, 21
Government, 21–41
Great
  Britain, 30, 32–35
  Poland Lakeland, 11
Gross domestic product (GDP), 43, 49
  per capita, 49

H
Hazards, 7
History, 21–41
  early, 21
Hitler, Adolph, 32, 71
  death of, 35
Holy Roman Empire, 21–23
  dissolution of, 28
Huns, 21

I
Immigrants, 23
Imports, 49
Independence, 32
Industry, 45–46, 49
  automotive, 45
  chemical, 46
  defense, 45
Infant mortality rate, 9
Islam, 9
Israel, 34
Italy, 32–35, 49

J
Jagiellonian
  dynasty, 25
  University (University of Kraków), 26, 27
Japan, 32–35
Jerusalem, 34

Jewish
  Cultural Festival, 77
  Quarter, 77
Jews
  extermination of, 33, 35
  migration of, 23, 24
  persecution of, 23
  protections for, 23, 24
  support of, 26
John
  III Sobieski, 26
  Paul II, Pope, 26, 38
Jura, 20

K
Kaliningrad Oblast, 7
Kazimierz Dolny, 60, 61
Kingdom of Poland, 22
Klopsiki w Śmietanie (Polish meatballs), 57
Kraków, 8, 13, 27, 34, 59, 60, 69, 74–75, 76, 77

L
Language, 9, 26–27
Laws, 23
Łazienki Palace, 71
Lendians, 21
Life expectancy, 9
Literacy rate, 9, 53
Literature, 27, 30, 58
  Romaniticist, 58
Lithuania, 7, 11, 25
  alliance with, 25
Lithuanians, 27
Little Poland, 13
Location, 7
Łódź, 69, 72–73
Lutherans, 25
Luxembourg, 41

93

INDEX

M
Maastricht Treaty, 41
Magdeburger Reiter, 22
Magyars, 21
Malbork, 62
    Castle, 62–63
Małysz, Adam, 53–54
Manufaktura, 73
Map, 6
Marienburg, 62
Masurian Lakeland, 11, 13
Matejko, Jan, 64, 65
Mazurka, 59
McKinsey report, 89
Merger Treaty, 41
Middle Ages, 21–24
Mieszko I, 22, 23
Migration rate, 9
Military, 45
Miłosz, Czesław, 58
Mizeria (cucumber salad), 57
Moniuszko, Stanisław, 58
Morawiecki, Mateusz, 88
Motława River, 80
Mountains, 12, 13
Mount Zion, 34
Music, 27, 58–59
    folk, 58, 59
    opera, 58

N
Napoleon. *See* Bonaparte, Napoleon
Napoleon Bonaparte (David), 28
Napoleonic era, 28, 30
National
    parks, 19

National
    Theater and Opera, 69
Nationalism, 28, 30, 65
NATO, 21, 39, 45
Natural gas, 43, 48, 84
Nazi Germany, 32–35, 67, 70
Neanderthals, 21
Netherlands, 41, 49
Nietoperek Bat Preserve, 19
Nobel Prize, 58, 60
Nobles, 23, 27
Nogat river, 62
Norway, 48

O
Obodrites, 21
Odra river, 14
Ogrodzieniec Castle, 20
Olympics, 54
Orthodox Christianity, 9
Otmuchów, 44, 86
Otto I, 21, 22
Ottoman Turks, 28
Ownership, state, 45

P
Palace of Culture and Science, 36
Paris, 30
Parliament, 25
Partitions, 28
Peasantry, 23, 27
People, 9, 53–66
Philharmonic National Orchestra, 69
Piotrkowska Street, 72
Plants, 17
Płaszów concentration camp, 34
Polanes, 21
Polish
    language, 9
    meatballs, 57
    people, 9
Polish-Lithuanian Commonwealth, 27, 28, 29
Polka, 59
Pomeranian Lakeland, 11
Population, 9
    age, 9
    density, 67, 69
    growth rate, 9
Ports, 50
Potatoes, 47
Poverty, 83
Poznań, 78–79
President, 37
Prime minister, 88
Princip, Gavrilo, 30
Privatization, 45
Protestantism, 9
Protestant Reformation, 25
Prussia, 28

Q
Q22 tower, 68
Quo Vadis (Sienkiewicz), 58

R
Raczki Elbląskie, 7
Radwar, 45
Recession, 43
Recipes, 57
Refugees, 83
Religion, 9
    freedom of, 25, 53
Rivers and waterways, 14

INDEX

Roman
    Catholicism, 9, 21–22, 23, 25, 27, 37, 53
    Empire, 21. *See also* Holy Roman Empire
Romanticism, 28, 30, 65
Royal
    Baths Park, 71
    Castle, 70
Russia, 7, 11, 28, 30, 32–35, 49, 83
    control by, 28
Rysy, 7

S
Schengen border rule, 39
Schindler, Oskar, 34
Schindlerjuden, 34
Schindler's List, 34
Sejm, 25
Self-Portrait (Matejko), 64
Serbia, 30
Services sector, 45
Shock therapy, 45
Sienkiewicz, Henryk, 58
Silesian
    language, 9
    people, 9
Slavic group, 21
Slovakia, 7, 11, 12, 14, 82
Slovak people, 27
Solidarity, 37
Solidarity (Solidarność), 42
Sorbonne, 60
Soviet Union, 8, 35
Sports, 53–54
St.
    Mary's Basilica, 76
    Stanislaus Church, 78

Stanisław II Augustus, 29
Stawa Mlyny, 10
Stews, 56
Sudeten Mountains, 13, 14
Sweden, 28
Świnoujście, 10, 43
Szczecin, 48
Szkoła podstawowa, 53
Szymborska, Wislawa, 26

T
Tannenberg, 63
Tatra
    Mountains, 12, 82
    National Park, 12
Taxes, 51
Technical University of Łódź, 72
Terrain, 7
Teutonic Knights, 52, 62
Thermal power, 85
Toruń, 52
Tourism, 59
Toyota, 46
Transportation, 49–50
Treaties of Rome, 41
Treaty of Paris, 41
Trees, 17
Tusk, Donald, 89

U
Ukraine, 7, 11, 25, 39
Ukrainian people, 9, 27
UNESCO World Heritage List, 71
United Kingdom, 49
University of Kraków, 26
University of Łódź, 72
Uplands, 13

Vistulans, 21
Volkswagen, 46

W
Walesa, Lech, 37
Warsaw, 11, 15, 35, 36, 50, 66, 69–71, 88
    Barbican, 69
    destruction of, 71
    Old Town, 66, 71
    Uprising, 70
    Uprising Monument, 67
Warta River, 78
Wawel
    Castle, 74–75
    Hill, 74
West Germany, 40, 41
White stork, 16, 17
Wind farms, 48, 86
Wisła River, 11, 14, 15, 60, 61, 69, 74
Władyslaw II Jagiello, 25, 74
Włodkowie Sulimczycy family, 20
Wojtła, Karol, 38
World Bank, 51
World War
    I, 30–32
    II, 32–35, 40, 66, 71

Z
Złoty, 49

95

Picture Credits

All images in this book are in the public domain or have been supplied under license by © Shutterstock.com. The publisher credits the following images as follows:

Page 8: Mykolastock, page 38: Gasper Furman, page 40: Roman Yanushevsky, page 44: Mariusz Szcygiel, page 48: Mike Mareen page 50: Nightman1965, page 54: Andry Yurlov, page 55: Magdalena Galkiewicz, page 59 De Visu, page 61: Patryk Kosmider, page 67: Meunierd, page 68: Udmurd, pages 72, 73: Mariold Anna S, page 77: Mikolajn.

Wikimedia Commons/Marek Mytnik

To the best knowledge of the publisher, all images not specifically credited are in the public domain. If any image has been inadvertently uncredited, please notify the publisher, so that credit can be given in future printings.

Video Credits

Page 12 STRATFORvideo: http://x-qr.net/1FXM
Page 22 Khey Pard: http://x-qr.net/1F2y
Page 46 TRT World: http://x-qr.net/1Fg5
Page 55 Ana Hribar: http://x-qr.net/1GeC
Page 68 Expedia: http://x-qr.net/1GP2

Author

Dominic J. Ainsley is a freelance writer on history, geography, and the arts and the author of many books on travel. His passion for traveling dates from when he visited Europe at the age of ten with his parents. Today, Dominic travels the world for work and pleasure, documenting his experiences and encounters as he goes. He lives in the south of England in the United Kingdom with his wife and two children.